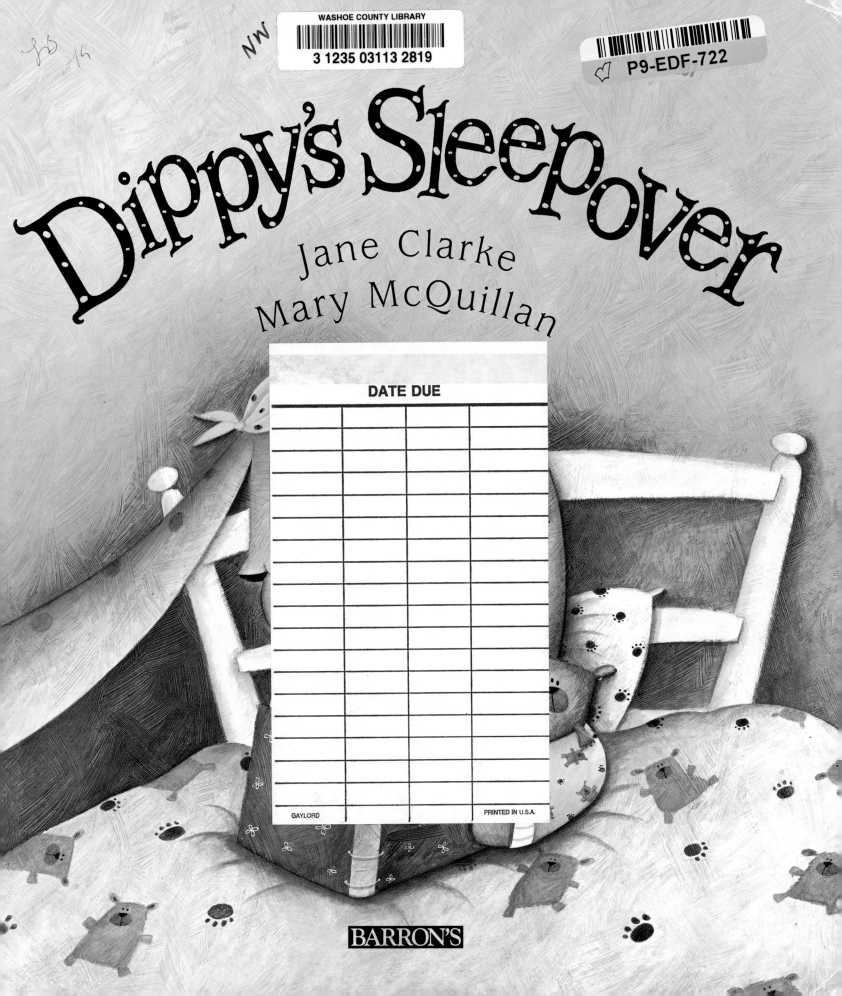

Dippy's Sleepover

Jane Clarke

Mary McQuillan

BARRON'S

For Avril with love – JC

For Will – MMcQ

First edition for the United States and Canada published in
2006 by Barron's Educational Series, Inc.

First published in Great Britain in 2006 by
Red Fox, an imprint of Random House Children's Books
Originated by THE BODLEY HEAD

Text copyright © Jane Clarke, 2006
Illustrations copyright © Mary McQuillan, 2006

The right of Jane Clarke and Mary McQuillan to be identified as the author and illustrator of this work
has been asserted in accordance with the Copyright, Designs and Patents Act, 1988.

Red Fox Books are published by Random House Children's Books
61-63 Uxbridge Road, London W5 5SA
A division of The Random House Group Ltd

All inquiries should be addressed to:
Barron's Educational Series, Inc.
250 Wireless Boulevard
Hauppauge, NY 11788
http://www.barronseduc.com

Library of Congress Control Number 2005930096

ISBN-13: 978-0-7641-3425-8
ISBN-10: 0-7641-3425-6

Printed in Singapore
9 8 7 6 5 4 3 2 1

On Tuesday after school, Dippy rushed home.
"Spike invited me to sleep at his house on Friday!"
he squeaked, wagging his tail excitedly.
"We'll watch *Scarysaurs Go Wild*
and eat popfern and . . ."

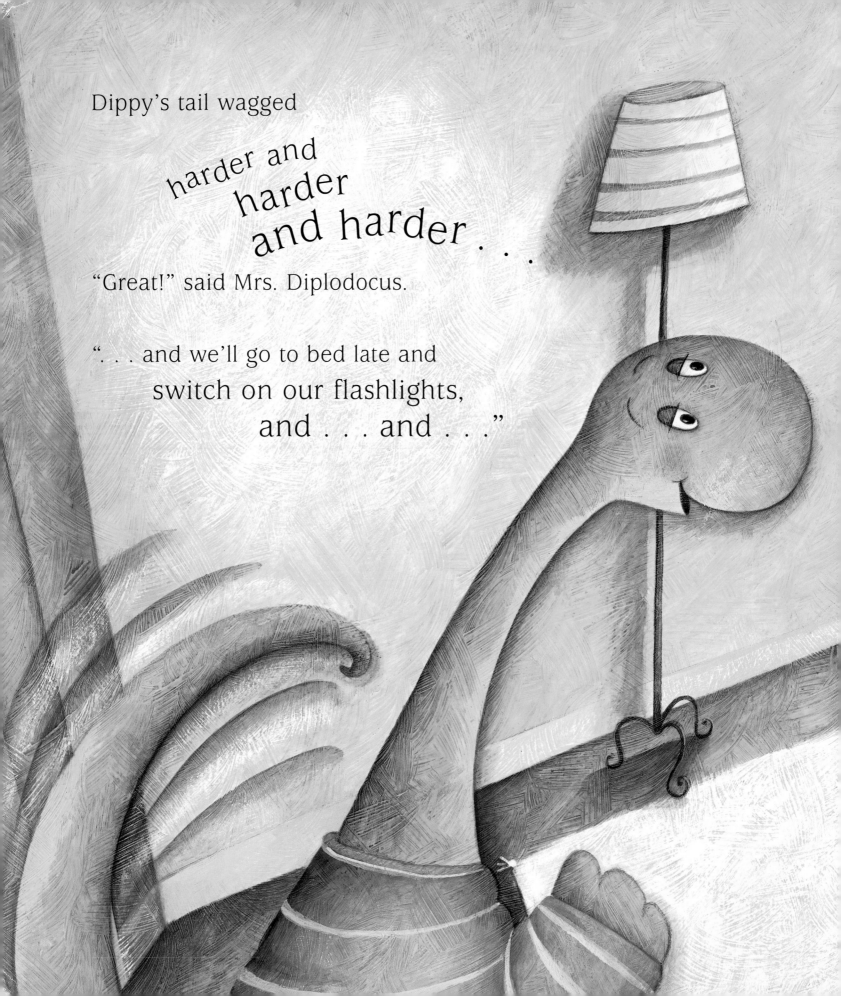

Dippy's tail wagged

harder and
harder
and harder . . .

"Great!" said Mrs. Diplodocus.

". . . and we'll go to bed late and
switch on our flashlights,
and . . . and . . ."

Dippy's tail stopped wagging.
"I can't go," he said sadly.
"Why not?" asked Mom.
"Because when I'm asleep,"
Dippy said, "I wet the bed."

Mrs. Diplodocus wrapped her long neck
around Dippy and gave him a hug.
"Lots of podlets wet the bed," she said.
"Mrs. Triceratops will understand.
She can put rubber sheets on
the mattress. I'll phone her."

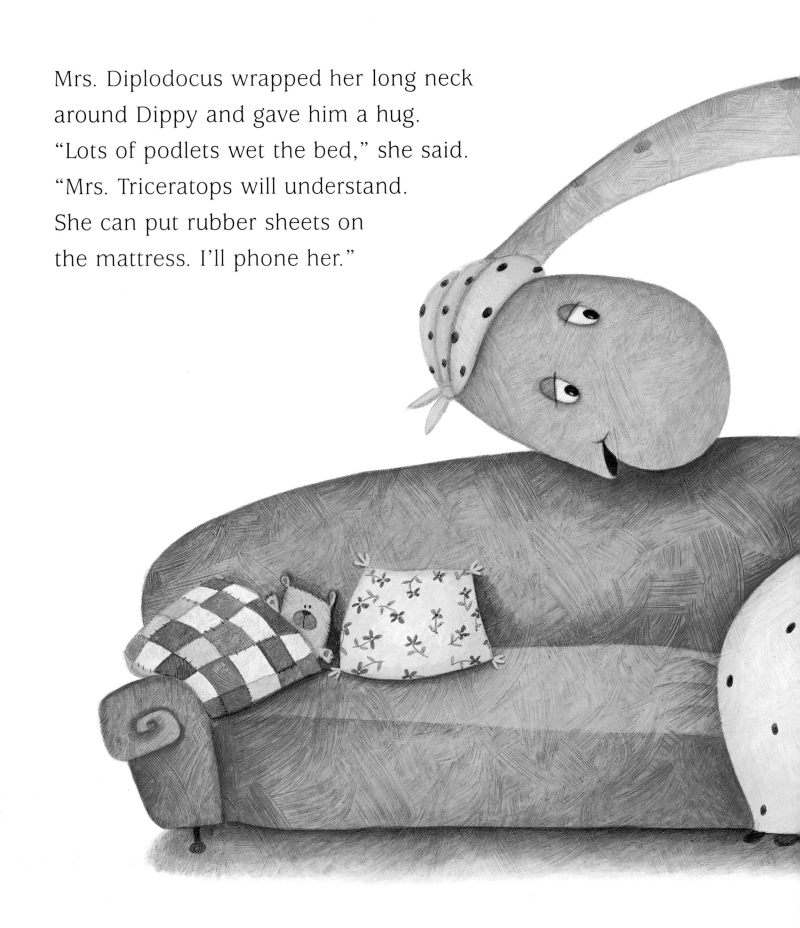

"Spike mustn't know
I wet the bed!"
said Dippy.

"I'll be dry
by Friday!"

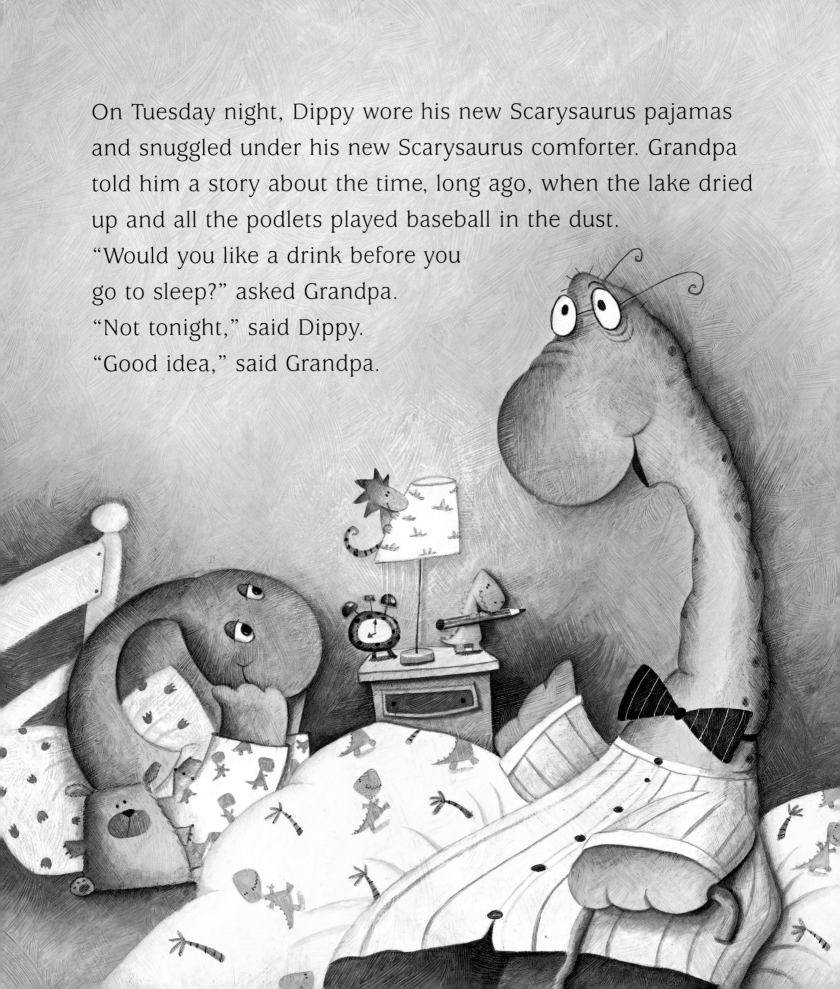

On Tuesday night, Dippy wore his new Scarysaurus pajamas
and snuggled under his new Scarysaurus comforter. Grandpa
told him a story about the time, long ago, when the lake dried
up and all the podlets played baseball in the dust.
"Would you like a drink before you
go to sleep?" asked Grandpa.
"Not tonight," said Dippy.
"Good idea," said Grandpa.

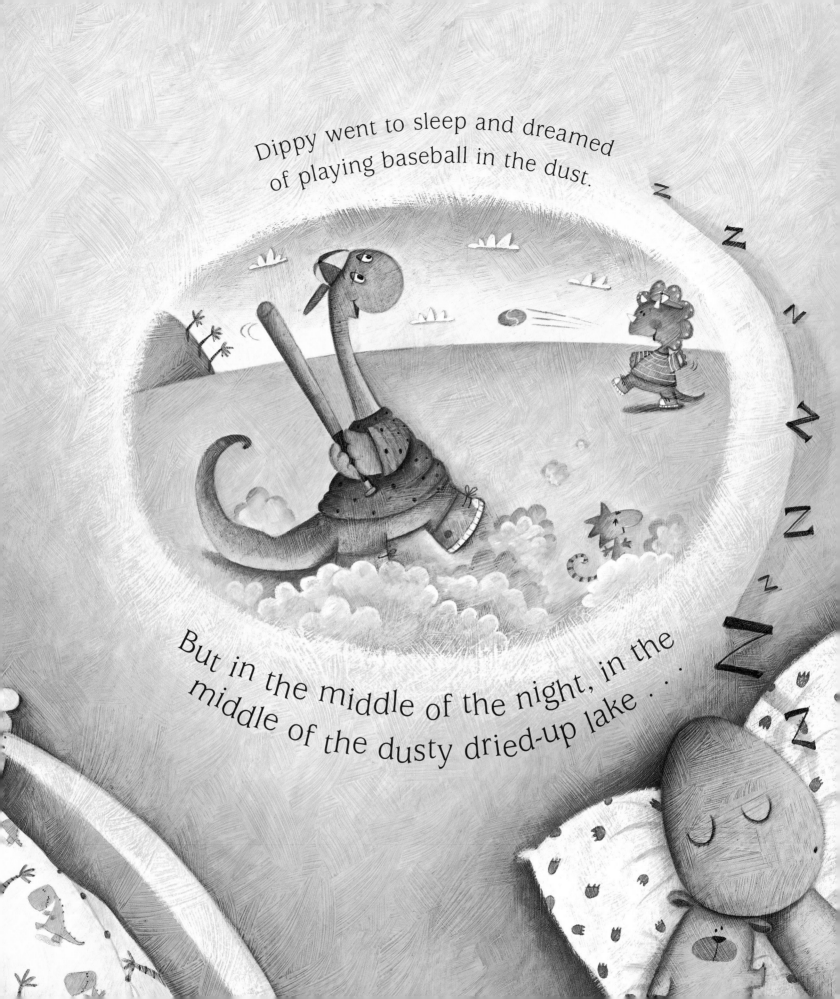

Dippy went to sleep and dreamed
of playing baseball in the dust.

But in the middle of the night, in the
middle of the dusty dried-up lake . . .

. . . a stream began to trickle . . . .

On Wednesday morning,
Mrs. Diplodocus changed the bedding.
"Friday will be here soon," she said.
"Let me phone Spike's mother."

"Spike mustn't know I wet the bed!"
said Dippy.

"I'll be dry by Friday!"

WED

On Wednesday night, Dippy wore his Little Pterrors pajamas and snuggled under his Little Pterrors comforter. Dad read him a story about a hot, dry desert where podlets played tag up and down the sand dunes.

"I'll go to the bathroom before you turn off the light," said Dippy. "Good idea," said Dad.

Dippy went to sleep and dreamed of playing tag up and down desert sand dunes.

But in the middle of the night, in the middle of the desert . . .

. . . a water hole began to fill . . .

On Thursday morning,
 Mrs. Diplodocus changed the bedding.
 "It's Friday tomorrow," she said.
 "I should phone Spike's mother."

"Spike mustn't know I wet the bed!"
said Dippy.

"I'll be dry by Friday!"

THUR

On Thursday night, Dippy had to wear his old cave bear pajamas
and snuggle under his old cave bear comforter, because everything
else was in the wash. Mom got out the album and they
laughed at the photo of Dippy buried in the sand.
"Wake me up when you go to bed," said Dippy,
"so I can go to the bathroom."
"Good idea," said Mom,
and she did.

Dippy went to sleep and dreamed
he was buried in the sand.

But in the middle of the night,
in the middle of the beach . . .

. . . the tide began to come in . . .

On Friday morning, Mrs. Diplodocus changed the
bedding. Then she packed Dippy's Scarysaurus
pajamas for him to take to Spike's house after school.
"I'm phoning Spike's mother now," she said,
but Mrs. Triceratops had already gone out.
"Phew!" Dippy said. "Spike mustn't know
I wet the bed!

I'll be dry
tonight!"

On Friday after school, Dippy had a
great time at Spike's house. Mrs. Triceratops
made them deep-fried ferns as a snack.
They watched *Scarysaurs Go Wild*
and ate popfern and drank firconeade.

"It's time to go to bed now," said Mrs. Triceratops.
"Would you like another drink?"
"No thanks," said Dippy and Spike together.

Dippy and Spike put on their matching
Scarysaurus pajamas and snuggled under their
matching Scarysaurus comforters with their cuddly
cave bears. Dippy was very tired, but he didn't
want to go to sleep in case he wet the bed.

"Let's stay awake all night!" he yawned.
"Good idea!" Spike yawned back.
They switched on their flashlights, but
soon their eyelids began to droop.

Dippy and Spike fell asleep and dreamed scary dreams about Scarysaurs.

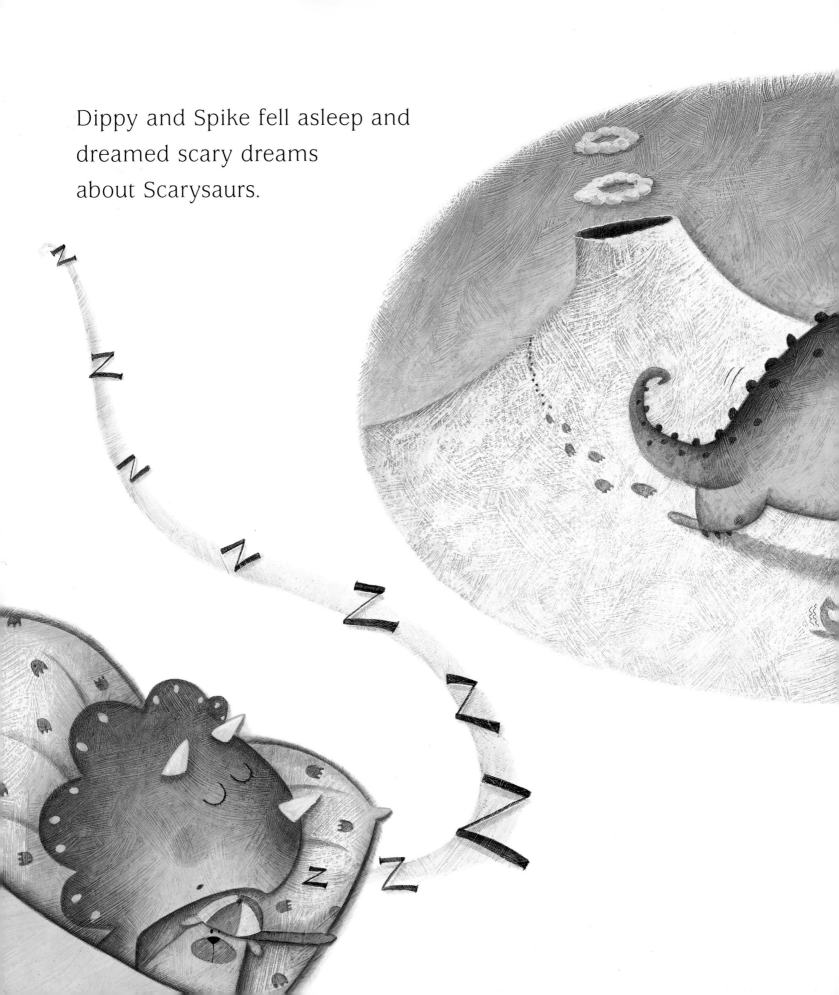

A huge Scarysaurus was chasing them through the snow. It was just about to catch them!

But in the middle of the night, in the middle of the volcano . . .

. . . the snow
began to melt . . .

On Saturday morning, Mrs. Triceratops
changed both sets of bedding.
"I didn't want you to know that I wet the bed!"
Dippy told Spike as a blush rippled down
his long neck.
"Well, *I* didn't want *you* to know
that I wet the bed," said Spike,
whose horn had gone all pink.

They looked at each other and smiled wobbly smiles.
"Don't worry about it," Mrs. Triceratops said.
"You'll grow out of it. Lots of podlets
wet the bed!"

"How did you get along at Spike's?"
Mom asked Dippy when he got home.
"It was great," said Dippy. "We watched
Scarysaurs Go Wild and ate popfern and . . ."
Dippy's tail
wagged
harder
and harder
and harder . . .

"And the bed . . . ?" asked Mom.

"Don't worry about that," said Dippy.

"Spike wets the bed, too!"

"Does he?" Mom smiled.

"Yes," Dippy said. "Lots of podlets wet the bed. We'll grow out of it."

"Of course you will," said Mom, giving him a huge hug.

On Saturday night Dippy
    fell into a deep sleep, and
        on Sunday morning . . .

Mrs. Diplodocus didn't have to change the bedding!